MW01245608

on the way back home

Stories from home, my way back

and the people I met along.

Lakshmy Das

XpressPublishing
An imprint of Notion Press

XpressPublishing

An imprint of Notion Press

No.8, 3rd Cross St, CIT Colony,
Mylapore, Chennai,
Tamil Nadu - 600004

First Published by Notion Press 2021
Copyright © Lakshmy Das 2021
All Rights Reserved.

ISBN 978-1-63781-908-1

to,

Ananth Vishnu, who always wanted me to write more.

This book wouldn't have come into being if the air in Kumily wasn't the same; if the hills were any different. This book wouldn't have come into being if Amma had not stood by me the way she does. This book wouldn't have come into being had the people in my life were any less kind.

This book owes Rose Taniya Joly for her brilliant editing skills and for constantly pushing me to complete it.

This book owes Karthika M for her beautiful illustrations that make the stories more alive.

This book owes Amrutha T R for giving form to the essence of the stories in this collection through the cover design.

And finally, this book owes it to coffee for always being there.

-Lakshmy Das

Contents

A Note to Remembrance

Each day we wake up to changes. At times, to the rays of a beginning. Sunny, bright, and beautiful. On other days, we wake up to a pour of purification. Doubtful, incomplete, yet worthy.

When speaking of changes, I should not miss to appreciate the dryness and the drought even while embracing a misty morning or a soulful sunset.

All such times of the year can be noted through the trees and the flowers if we are gentle enough to believe that existence of every sort solely blooms from the depth of the roots.

Home here is the inevitable ingredient which makes even the unpredictable changes worth the welcome.

These stories come from nowhere else but from the heart of the author herself. She picked them under a tree, from a dry leaf, and a fallen flower along the ways from her misty native, where she walked most of her life. Some she borrowed from people who carried love, people like her mother who would conveniently scold and feed at the same time, her father who couldn't care more in the most careless way.

Gathered from the most intimate incidents, each story takes us miles away but always urges to understand the most beautiful of journeys occur while traveling back home.

It is that understanding which we all miss at times. We are somehow in a hurry to abandon our native, ashamed to accept the roots for some reason unknown. Is it in the nature of humans to naturally leave behind the streams to find the ocean or is it the social construct that knowingly or unknowingly forces us to flee? I do not know or rather I'm not yet there to give an answer. But let me tell you this for sure, even though home can be something that we carry within ourselves, there must be a physical space-

a tree, a shade, a fruit, a shadow that waits through times for us to come back and settle down.

'on the way back home' is a solicitude to be remembered.

To not hesitate to be broken.

To find a smile in the smallest of flowers.

To keep a tear apart for the strangest of reasons,

and above all to believe that belonging is the most adorable way of praying.

"Once you find home, then time is just a thought. And once you find God, then even those thoughts die. I don't really know how old I am, I just know that I am home, in the lap of my master, in a shelter that will never throw me out." {Churuli}

-Archit Ameya

the writer just wants to remember this:

"listen to the river, Siddhartha."

i hope you come back to these stories on days you
want to remember home,

to remember love,

and to remember to walk with yourself.

with love,

lakshmy

home

I woke up to a memory today, and the taste of the water from that well lingered on my tongue for a while.

Once again, I was standing before that small hut. The dark jungle that surrounded the wooden structure seemed a little too eerie at first; those giant trees did not allow much light to seep through. But then, the light that I found in her eyes made the eeriness bearable. She came out when she sensed my presence in the courtyard, she had her child in her arms as she walked out through that small door. She was breastfeeding the little one, and when she looked at me, standing almost lost, she couldn't help but smile. I asked her if she could give me some water. She nodded and smiled again.

She turned around gently and put the child to sleep on the palmyra mat that was laid out on the verandah. She covered the little one in a rug, and then arranged her saree and walked to the well. She walked as though she knew I would come. She was smiling to herself for some reason. She smiled as though she knew that a lost, environmental researcher would knock at her door, asking for water, and stand puzzled.

As she walked to the well, I looked around. I could sense the feeling of fear that was gripping me. I was alone, my team was at another part of the settlement and I had no means to communicate with them; my phone was dead. But despite the fear, I could feel that I was slowly being moved by something stronger than my fear. And I can never put that in words. What I felt might be closer to what the Buddha said - "every moment is purification." But even then, I cannot tell you what that meant at that given point. Perhaps I was overwhelmed by the stillness that I felt there. I do not know.

The stone structure that surrounded the well was almost completely covered with mosses and ferns. This piece of land has pepper as the main crop. The vines wrapped the trees like pretty decorations; they held the people together as well. There were rare plants that grew in the wilderness outside her hut; there was a string of hearts that found its home around her well. But everything there was soaked in a certain silence that was beyond my understanding. She paused for a second and slowly leant forward to get hold of the rope. The well was deep; her movements echoed from it. The well didn't seem to like the intrusion. It made noises similar to a child that is disturbed in sleep; it made angry noises. And as she pulled the rope, the pulley made a sound that startled me, putting an end to the train of thoughts. The silence there was so full that a murmur felt like an explosion, and as she fetched the water from the well, the sound of the splashes hit my eardrums like loud metal clangs.

She gestured to me to come closer, and I did. I cupped my hands and drank from the old iron bucket. The water tasted pristine; the taste of rust did surface, but this water tasted nothing as I had ever tasted before. It somehow tasted ancient, it tasted as if it belonged to a different space and time. But it was just water and it felt stupid to think so much about it. I laughed at myself, letting the guard down finally. And suddenly, her presence overwhelmed me like nothing I had ever known before. I didn't know what was happening to me, it was too profound to be real. She was simply standing there, lost in her own thoughts; but for me, she seemed to exist in a realm that was hidden from the outside world. She reminded me of something that I had long forgotten, and that trembled me.

I couldn't bear it anymore; what was happening to me was too intense, and I pulled myself together quickly. I had to. Again, the fear got the better of me. I thanked her in a rush and walked to the verandah to collect my bag. The child was awake, but it didn't cry. I smiled at the little one.

And then, I smiled at her.

Her slender figure stood by the door, watching me walk back. As I reached the other side of the mud road, I turned back to look at her once more. And I took a deep breath.

Suddenly it hit me; the randomness of everything that was in place and the inherent chaos that holds it all together. And at that moment, all my questions and answers melted away. All the answers that made everything sensible seemed too silly. And the questions smirked at me. They laughed at my ignorance. At that moment, everything blurred- the sounds of the forest faded away. I felt still once again.

I took another deep breath. The cool air burnt my nostrils. And for one last time, I looked at her. She smiled again.

Those few seconds with her; the smell of the damp earth, the dull murmur of those giant trees, the smoke from her hut, the little one's giggle, the taste of that water, and the answers that she hid in her eyes, they somehow stripped my being naked without seeking my permission. And I couldn't help but bare myself before that unknown woman; before the vastness of that jungle. For me, life has been a silent seeking after that day. Though I can never really tell you what I seek, or what actually happened to me that day, but I can tell you that she was a reminder that I needed. A gentle reminder to look within and find home. And I am glad I got lost that day.

churuli

"Time is relative," remarked Churuli. She isn't a physicist. In fact, Churuli has never been to school. She hasn't heard of Einstein. Come to think of it, not even about the Mahatma. Her theory of time came from the tree. She used to say that it spoke to her when they were alone. She lived near the Banyan tree for years, making it her home while protecting it with her subtle presence. Both the tree and the woman stood as the centre of our small community.

The banyan was old, and like the earth upon which it thrived, it was home to many. From nestlings to Nilgiri Langurs, the tree sheltered all those who sought her. Just like Churuli.

Churuli was over eighty for sure, but no one really knew her exact age or her origins. She used to wear a saree, but her style of draping it was unusual; she wore it without a blouse. On most days, I used to see her with a brown blanket, something she held very precious. And when her blanket gets torn, someone from the village would buy a new one for her. The thing is, she just had to mention something and our people would run to get it for her. She was the grandmother of the village. Everyone loved her that way. In fact, if she had agreed, our people were ready to take her home and look after her. But she never left that old hut of hers, the one beside the banyan tree, which was her home. The hut was also home to a few stray dogs. She used to feed them with the little she earned as alms.

She used to tell us things that never made sense to us as kids. Nevertheless, she told them. Maybe she knew that one day we would remember those words, like how I do now.

"Once you find home, then time is just a thought. And once you find God, then even those thoughts die. I don't really know how old I am, I just know that I am home, in the lap of my master, in a shelter that will never throw me out."

The last time we spoke, she told me that her God was the tree itself. And I couldn't help but wonder – how could a tree be someone's God? How could she believe in a thought that was so plain? But I wished that I could feel that way about something, at some point at least. I wished that I could trust an intangible force so deeply, so intensely.

Churuli was dear to the whole village, but she was particularly dear to us children. And we have heard the best stories from her, munching on things that she had prepared for us. She would go into the forest and fetch all that she could find to feed us. Guavas, mangoes, mulberries, and when it was the season, the jackfruit. She would clean the jackfruit, remove the seeds, and keep it outside her hut in a plate. And as we ran back from school, her humble hut was our dearest stop. She took care of our hunger, both of our stomach and of our soul.

If we were lucky enough, Churuli would sing a folk song for us. The songs that praised the creator and the songs that spoke about love were her dearest. And every time love came up, she used to smile wide.

I always used to wonder who her lover would have been. I was always curious to know about her past back then. But these days, after knowing a bit more about love, all I wonder is how one could learn to love like her. Her love gave her joy. It set her free. And I really don't know if I can ever do that anymore.

"Chinnamma," she called me one day as I was roaming near her hut. Saddened by the loss of my father, I was trying all that I could to make some sense of life.

"You should not let the world weigh you down. Nor your losses. Your father is at rest. You should know that. You needn't worry your heart about what death is. When you are ready, that knowledge will not sit heavy upon your chest."

Churuli took my face in her palms and continued.

"Now you must grow. And one day, like this tree, become home to souls. Become their dearest home. And for that, grow your roots stronger."

Churuli then suddenly stopped. She looked up at

the sky and hurried me.

"It is about to rain my child. Get back home. Come back when you feel like it."

I looked at her frail body. She was sitting still. She did not hurry me because she saw the rains coming, there was something else. I didn't know what it was, but she had a dull smile on her lips. And I obeyed her.

In fact, that day I obeyed her totally. I turned out to become home to a few people. I have also become a writer now.

And every time I look back, Churuli sits on that old cot before her hut, smiling at me as I walked back. A few seconds with her that I still do not understand totally, steered me along a path that has been unforgettable.

I believe that there are these very few moments in our life when logic takes a backseat, and those moments leave us changed. Be it love, be it devotion, be it madness, be it a rather unexpected journey or a rare finding; certain moments change the course of our life. If we are lucky, that moment will define the way we look at life. It will change us into what we never thought possible. A moment like that will leave us hopeful and hopeless, simultaneously. And from that point, what we were doesn't matter anymore. We look around. We see. We hear. And we listen, finally. We learn to listen without wanting to agree. Without wanting to reply. We simply listen.

For the first time that day, I could feel Churuli's voice ringing in my ears. I was listening, taking it all in. I listened to her just the way we listen to the rain, to the murmurs of the tree. We don't search for answers there, we needn't actually. Life is never about the answers in fact, maybe that was all that Churuli was trying to tell me. And she was true, it can never be about an answer. It is far too profound to be limited to an answer. She breathed this truth in her very being.

Churuli died a few days back. And I felt that I should note this down. Maybe as a memoir. Or as a reminder. I don't know. The hut she lived in would soon be gone as well. Maybe the tree too. I don't want her to fade away completely. So, this note.

Sometimes I think that Churuli was the God who she used to talk about. In fact, it wasn't the tree that was the home, it was her. She saved it. It was not the other way around. Now that I think about it, I am sure that the tree would have bowed down to her every day.

the priest

The boy was seventeen. Dark skinned, lean, and an introvert. He wore a dull smile on his lips, the kind of smile that made people wonder, the kind that made people worry. Despite all the losses that he had been through, his heart was still hopeful; the smile was but a reflection of that. When Father George asked him to come over and help him out at the church, Alex never really expected what he would have had to witness there. Literally, life was giving him strange surprises again and again.

Graambi is a small town with bare minimum facilities. A large part of the population resides in and around the town, leaving behind large stretches of agricultural land at the outskirts. These lands that made them rich in the past were places of the visit now; the workers were in charge of things. The labourers did the cultivation, they managed all that needed to be managed and no one intervened, except when the produce was ripe enough for the market. That was when the owners paid a detailed visit to their lands, which produced the best cardamom in Kerala.

Alex belonged to one such family of workers. Neither of his parents lived to witness the new church that had been constructed for the people of Graambi; they surrendered their lives to cancer much before the cure became cheap. They left together, leaving him all alone; a gap of six months is not that huge after all. No one bothered to take care of the boy who had just finished school. No one thought of sending him to college or at the very least, about his food. He found himself a small job, but he knew he had to do something to escape his situation. Until Father George visited the tea stall, he had no idea of how to save himself. But Father brought in hope. Father could help him find education- that made his heart jump with joy.

With the new church and the new vicar in town, the lives of our people began to see a new dimension. The vicar was a man of surprises, and that meant a lot of changes. Some that they weren't ready for. He was not a man of soft and gentle gestures, rather he was someone who knew how to kill a boar in one blow. Father asked Alex to hop into the jeep. Alex did. The village praised the vicar for his great heart. Indeed, his heart was great. There is no doubt in that.

Father George was a big man. He was six-feet tall; a well-built man with a strong sense of humour and justice. This amused almost everyone. He was a peoples' person too; the kind of human being who put his people before himself. He rode a Royal Enfield, the roar of which resounded everywhere in that small town. He had strange interests for a priest to keep; his biggest passion was hunting and his biggest craze was for the rifles. He hated people who softened themselves to please others. He was the kind who believed that human beings are meant to be fierce and for sure; one could feel the fire in his eyes every time he stood up for what he felt was right.

His love for the rifles remained a secret between the man himself and the fellow who purchased them for him. But the night he took Alex to his quarters, the boy found his collection of rifles only to get a fever the next day. Over the days, his sleepless nights were filled with conversations that he overheard. Conversations that made him wonder what he had gotten himself into.

"Binu, you won't believe what I managed to get last day! A porcupine! That too from twenty feet away!"

Father beamed as the voice on the other side replied. Alex took a deep-silent-breath in and wondered what he would have done with that animal.

"I don't think it is that bad after all. See Binu, you are hunted in the human form by all those who pretend to love you. The politicians hunt you. The police and the court will hunt you if someone smart can turn some shreds of evidence against you. So, if a human being can hunt his fellow brother, does this really harm the ecosystem that much? No, it doesn't. It can't. Hunting is in our genes. If we don't take the rifle, our minds will find other means to hunt. I would rather hunt with my guns than with any other means."

Silence again.

Alex listened to the sound of the cicadas and the leaky tap. He could feel his chest growing heavy. He didn't know if he really wanted education anymore. He was terrified.

Something flashed in his mind and replaced the image of the dead porcupine. The dog that bit two of the school children yesterday was found dead in its owner's compound. It was heard that the dog was shot dead. The people here had a rather unusual silent discussion on the matter and the discussions ended unusually fast. His eyes glowed in the dark; the complexity of the situation was too much for him to hold within. He was a young boy, very new to this strange world. He felt a chill down his spine. The priest had brought many changes to their simple lives in fact.

The vicar was a strange man in fact, but no one knew if he was really the monster that Alex thought he was. Strange people have an unusual impact on the society they live in. That is true. Sometimes they even become the law. Sometimes they become home to a few. And sometimes. they change the way others view kindness. In the end, what they do is to silently change the basics.

Alex was worried about his future. He ought to be. He didn't know if he was safe. Although he knew that Father wouldn't harm him, he didn't know if hc could risk it. The vicar wasn't a bad man, in fact, he had a great heart. He just wasn't the usual good.

The man who had molested Meenu, who was hardly seven years old, got shot in his leg the other day. The man who traded dog meat with beef, found his buffaloes missing quite a number of times until he quit his business and left the village. Things like this kept happening in Graambi, but no one bothered to ask how or why; everyone just knew that they should behave themselves. In a way, the vicar just made the place safer than any other place nearby. But Alex lived in the room next to the one that had the collection of guns, and he had a different opinion on matters. Maybe a change of room would have helped him to get a different perspective. I don't know.

the memory of love

We don't always remember love with happiness. We often remember it with pain. At least for my generation of people it is so. For us, love has been about survival; a journey that we made to forget the pangs of struggle and repression. For us, love was solace, and therefore, the most treasured kindness we ever received.

As I write this, the rain falls upon the land as if it is in a rage to end it all. The howling of the wind is louder than usual. The monsoon is quiet on its own terms these days. The earth has forgotten its old ways I suppose. It no longer rains on the Chithira Pournami[1]. Things have changed.

The paddy fields opposite our house are overflowing; the many channels of water have filled the cervices of the planet and it looks like she is unable to contain it within her. The wind keeps splashing rain upon my face. It feels really good to be back home. It is years later that I sit by this window again, but the rain, just like it used to drench my

---

[1] Chithira Pournami is observed on the day of the full moon in the Tamil month of Chithirai or Chaitra, which falls in the month of April or May in the Gregorian calendar.

being years before, did its job quite the same. I just wonder where he would be right now!

Whenever I think of him, what I remember the most is the Arjun tree standing tall in the mist. It might be a little weird to remember a tree as the sole memory of love; but for me, our love is best remembered as a living, rooted presence. The tree has always bore flowers that looked faded in the mist, often it was hard to figure out the leaves from the flowers in one look. Whenever the tree flowered, Kumily would be covered in the mist. Sometimes I think the earth wants to hide the beauty of the tree from those who do not value that sight enough. For us, our life was tied to the tree; the colours of its flowers were etched in our souls. The tree was a living being in our story.

We studied in the only college that was functional in our small town. It was a parallel college, the one where you study and write the exam under private registration in the university. It was quite a big deal to have a college to go to. It was a privilege, to be able to be involved in politics, in student movements, when most families couldn't afford their children's basic education. Our principal, who was a revolutionary himself, did not teach us just academic lessons. He instilled revolution and kindness in our very cells. If not for that campus, I would have lived a very predictable life. That campus changed my life.

Lal was my senior in college. He was the kind of person who was always burning with the spirit of revolution. Every time I think about him, his determined yet calm eyes come to the forefront. His presence; the very strength of his presence, still keeps my heart warm. He did not win my love, he rather moved my being into becoming love that was more than myself. And that was profound. For him, the revolution wasn't any different from love. He believed in both and that was the kind of strength that I wanted beside me. For life.

Today when we talk about Communism, all that we think about is the politics and the power-play involved in the organised political party. These days, people in politics rarely think about their fellow human beings, the marginalised, or the weak. Those who do think, are often purchased by the powerful in the business of politics. But for us, that was not the case. We believed in a fraternity. Our lives were aligned with the idea of living for others. A part of us lived for the community, and that was the best part of our lives.

Our love was built on the ideals of camaraderie; we were comrades for life, people who were willing to give themselves and everything they had for the revolution. And we loved the same way as well, we were willing to risk it all. But time has its ways on everything, and all that remains of that great love story is the tree; everything else fell off in the name of sacrifice. Sometimes, what you believe in eats you from the inside. Sacrifice is one such idea!

The other day I saw my daughter taking a photograph of the tree. She thinks it looks beautiful. She took that picture to send it to her friends in the city. Appu enjoys these short trips we make around the world, but this is the first time I have taken her to my hometown. I have never told her about Lal. I wonder how she would see it, her mother's lost love! She asked me if I knew what the tree was called. I smiled and told her that it is called the 'Tree of Love'. She was annoyed at my answer. She rolled her eyes, dismissed my bad joke, and walked away. I am glad she didn't ask me why I said so.

Like I said, the tree stands as the symbol of our love. And much like the tree, we shed our leaves and the dear flowers when we knew that it had to be done. We never said goodbye to each other; the flowers never say goodbye to the tree when it is time to leave. We knew that we wouldn't forget the love that made us grow. And like the earth that remembers the roots in her being, our love remains in us as a very dear memory.

We still talk to each other when we cross paths, silently saying a 'lalsalam' that crept into our blood long back. He has aged much; his hair all grey. Mine are still black though, and he makes fun of that every time; he strongly believes that I colour them and thinks that it is against the natural order of things. He still doesn't wear a watch.

It has been almost twenty years since we separated, and I had believed that the love we shared had been pushed to the sides we rarely visited. But one day, when we met at a common gathering, I realised that what I buried was somehow still not dead. That day, he sat with Appu and started talking to her. And when I went over to them, he smiled like the old times and told her, out of nowhere, that there is a journey that we had planned to take. And that, if there is a next time, we will. Appu, who was thoroughly confused, looked at me for a reply, but my face had already become pale. I could actually hear my heartbeats as he said those words, and my mind went back to that classroom where our laughter echoed. I sighed. The questions from Appu weren't even registering in my head, for all I could hear was his voice gently reminding us all, that 'of all things, love should give us hope.'

maruthan

There are some stories that we always want to share. Those exciting adventures that no one else would have ever had or the ones that had a huge impact on our lives, and thus shaped us. Some stories are so important that we believe they shouldn't die with us, and then there are some, which we would want to be buried with us.

Most of the stories that I have heard are stored in my head with the image of a fire and a bunch of people sitting around it. I have, in my head, a lot of them.

Appa, my father, had a habit of singing stories of the tribe. He would sing aloud the tales of the great tribe leaders with his eyes burning brighter than the fire before him. The pride which flowed in his veins was far more intoxicating than the alcohol within. He would, with his songs, often wake the souls that rested in the sacred grove of the village. He was always proud of our generation; the first set of people that went to school. But he despised those who refused the tradition. The Government Tribal School, which taught us letters and math, was seen with much reverence, but what they taught were never above the truths of our clan. Our fathers kept their heads low and dhotis down while speaking to our teachers; the teachers were that important to them. Schooling was an option to walk out of the customs. But then, even after having had the privilege of flying away, none of us ever did. The soil that we walked upon was too precious to be left behind for mere material gains.

Of the hundreds of stories that were heard and the hundreds forgotten, the one that changed my life was that of an old man. He was fifty-four years old when we killed him. Some stories have in them a fire that doesn't die, a fire that sometimes kills.

Maruthan was a silent man, 'poisonously' silent in my Appa's words. His head was always low; his eyes, lifeless during the day. It was on one of the full moon days that Appa told us about Maruthan. He was drunk as usual, but that day he had a strange look on his face. The face of a man whose deepest fears had turned true, and that made me listen to him rather carefully.

Maruthan was born to Lakka, a villager who married a man from the outside. No one ever heard him speak, and thus no one was sure if he was from Tamil Nadu or some other part of the country. And the mystery about the man deepened when he left Lakka, a few days after the boy was born. Lakka raised him well, but in her struggle to feed the child she forgot that he needed to be taught how to think and act. Like a wild animal, he grew up on his own terms and soon became a threat to the entire womenfolk of the tribe.

There existed a custom in our village that insisted our women to stay in a separate hut during their menstrual cycle. This hut would be a little farther from the homes, and they hardly had a proper door. The women would be given food there, during all four days, and on the fourth day of their cycle, they could come out and take a bath. This custom had to come to an end when two of our women were found raped inside these huts. And one dead. Like always, terrible things come out to light only when they become unmanageable.

It was Maruthan who attacked our women. What he did to them was not just sexual abuse but life-threatening atrocities that left them wanting nothing but death. But this never came out, as the women were not sure who did this to them at night. Out here, once the lamp is turned out, it means darkness till morning. The criminal was identified only on the day Periayappa followed him to Amutha's house; Amutha had just lost her husband to malaria.

Maruthan always attacked the vulnerable. And Periyappa, who is my Appa's elder brother, followed him from the toddy shop. Periyappa somehow felt that this guy was related to these crimes. And he got the intuition that if he was the criminal, he would attack Amutha that day or soon. Periyappa confirmed that the criminal was Maruthan, when he found the stick that he forced into our woman's genitals, after raping them, right outside Amutha's house. He was captured and sent to jail the next day, but the man was released a year later. There wasn't much evidence against him. Everyone thought that he wouldn't commit the crimes again, but this time the attack took the life of Paattima, my grandmother, who was seventy-nine, and the life of a thirteen-year-old, who often walked with me to the school. The last time he attacked, the pain subsided way too early than it should have; nothing was done to prevent his crimes. The people didn't know that the law could only keep the killer away for a year. We should have done something better.

Maruthan was not part of our lives up until that day when Appa spoke to us about what he feared about that man; about what he did to our grandmother, who was walking back from the temple when he attacked her. For us, he was but a poor fellow, who walked silently across the street with sugar and oil for his family. He was just a living being, who did not take up a space in the daylight. But from that night, something burned in my cells; the fire that the tale set in me was fierce enough to plan an attack on him. Perhaps what fuelled my anger was what I would lose if he was out there healthy and free; I could lose my sister, even my mother or my aunts. And that was the fear that let Appa share this story with us, even though we were all quite young back then. I wasn't yet a man before my Appa, but he had to save the women of his community.

We all had found jobs to support our families by then. All of us who studied in the school together kept our friendship strong with frequent meetings at the school ground. It used to be all fun, these meetings. We would talk endlessly about our jobs, our lives, and our romances. But that day, the air was serious and tense. No one smiled; our eyes burned with anger. Revenge had to be taken; Maruthan had to be stopped. Our plan was to never let him walk out and ruin the lives of our women and children. And we planned to break the bones of his legs, the ones that let him walk miles at night, hunting down our women. But some plans fail; some turn out to be what we never think about- for better or for worse is a matter of debate.

The nights here are very special. Even with a full-moon above, the trees never allowed much light to come down. It was always dark for a killer to hide well. And this time there were nine killers, all set to attack one man- just one man, who was equipped with nothing but a stick he got handy for his next victim. Vishal hit Maruthan's head from behind and we all moved into the scene, watching the man slowly fall down. To our surprise, he didn't try to resist us; all he did was to look up at the moon and smile. His smile provoked us even more and someone stabbed him on his foot with the knife. Others hit him with whatever weapon they had at hand. Our plan was to break his leg, to stop him from committing more crimes, but the cut on his ankle was deeper than what we had expected it to be, and seeing that the blood wouldn't stop, it was me who carried him on my shoulders and ran to the hospital. We never wanted to kill him. But he died. Fate does have a way of making us feel guilty for the plans she executes. Maruthan died at our hands on that full moon night. He had left before we reached the hospital. Everyone, except his son, knows that we are the people who killed him. I don't know if the little boy, who smiles at me every other day, would understand that guilt could be felt even after doing the right thing.

cheeniyamma

Cheeniyamma is sixty-two. She is my father's elder sister.

"Mary, I have brought some tapioca chips for the kids. Take this and give me the pain oil. The bus leaves soon. I have to rush."

Her frail voice was capable of making my mother jump up from the floor where she sat cleaning the rice bought from the ration shop. She is the only person in my father's family who my mother doesn't hate. In fact, my mother is very fond of her. Cheeniyamma drops by whenever she pays a visit to her childhood friend who lives nearby. Her friend is bedridden, a cancer survivor who lost her leg to the battle. Although it is hard for Cheeniyamma to carry heavy things, she makes sure that her best friend gets a decent supply of health mix powder to keep her going strong. She prepares it on her own. She calls it the 'divine mix'. Cheeniyamma visits Laly chechi[2] every two weeks and along with the health mix, she supplies a decent supply of emotional support to keep her friend's mind even stronger.

Their friendship is an old one, dating back to the

_____

[2] chechi refers to elder sister, someone older in age.

times when people had to work hard to keep themselves alive. They are the people who came to the hills as little children with their parents; parents fought the wild and the unknown to build a life here. There is nothing poetic about the struggle for the one who goes through it. And perhaps, the only thing that struggle gives us is the ability to endure more of it, which is very evidently visible in their lives. Their friendship is about survival; being there for each other is what saved them. They have lived through wild animal attacks, landslides, illnesses that took the lives of their dear ones, hunger, and betrayals. They have buried their parents; some of them, even their children, and they have fed a hundred mouths out of their kindness. They have been through it all, together. Things that we can't even imagine. Now you know what gives her the strength to carry that heavy big-shopper all the way up to her friends' house.

I don't recognise her voice very particularly. I find her voice much like the voice of every other old woman I have heard; feeble yet high pitched, slightly disturbing to the listener with those frequent inhalations, which reminds one of the asthmatic patients in hospital wards. She was thin, bent, and pale. But her soul, like the mountains we wake up to, has always been mighty and forever alive, despite the years that have gone by. Clad in her *Chatta*[3], which

---

[3] Chatta (or Chatta and Mundu) is a traditional attire worn by the women of the Christian population of the region

often bears the stains of the thousand things that she carried in her Pavithra Jewellery bag, she is stronger than most of the adults I have known. By strength, I mean both the physical and the mental strengths. She would walk miles, carry a big-shopper full of things for the different people she knew, and eat nothing but a snack leftover from the day before or a serving of tapioca and 'mulak-pottichathu', a chutney made of chilly and onion. She consumed, with her failing lungs, a much lesser amount of oxygen than most others, and with her gentle existence, she took up the very same space that cardamom scent took up in our homes. It would feel too weird when that presence is absent.

"Annammo, come out and get this oil. Your husband has been asking me for ages. It's just now that Mary could get it ready."

I could hear her voice from the other side of the road, full of concern and love, which I believe is a natural consequence of having spent a lifetime for others. She became a widow at the age of twenty-six and having lost her only child a year before that, she had no other option but to take destiny head-on. She still talks about her husband and how inhumanly strong he was; tales of his adventures and the places she had been with him. The feeling of love hasn't eroded from her heart after all these years. She has lived alone after losing her family, and her loneliness has given her a spirit that looks out for all those in need of help.

"How is your daughter's life there? Are they expecting a child any time soon?"

Joppan, who is also a distant relative, was at the other side of the road. He gestured a no.

The leaves of the giant jackfruit tree in his courtyard shivered as Joppan fell an unripe fruit for Cheeniyamma. She smiled as she knew that Chackochan's wife, who was seven months pregnant, would love to have it. Cheeniyamma memorises the likes and dislikes of her people much like a mother. It aches her poor heart to not do something for the people who expect from her; be it just bringing a piece of the Christmas cake or a root that helps in hair growth. I still remember how she walked over a mile to the old church with Joppan's help, and from there, all the way up to the estate, searching for that root among the thorny bushes. She once went all the way to Idukki to get the Gerbera seeds my mother had asked for. Mind you, that's a three hours journey one side. Though she doesn't travel alone these days, she would, if asked by someone, arrange the bus driver to fetch the things they want. She takes care of everyone as if it is her duty. And it looks as though someone sent her to our place so that no one feels alone.

Cheeniyamma packed the jackfruit in the same old big-shopper. The dirt-stained shopper looked as though it would burst and the lady carrying it looked as though she would fall; the weight pulled her left shoulder down but it couldn't weigh down the spirit she carried within. Cheeniyamma walked another mile without any qualms. As I said, stronger than most of us, she still carries a deep sense of tireless love within her- something that is enough to take her places.

I wonder how life here would be without the presence of this old woman. Though it is unkind of me to think so, somehow every single time I see people expect their life to be touched by this sixty-two-year-old lady, I simply wonder. Maybe the women should start preparing their children's favourite snack themselves. Maybe the girls should become free to try the hair oils they see in the advertisements. I don't know, I just wonder.

Maybe the big-shopper and what it carried to each home would be deeply missed. And I am not sure how the person will be missed, as people often forget a lot of things and a lot of people. I just know that a part of me will always look out for her voice from the other side of the road. A part of me will remember her every time I see kindness in the world.

the game

Amma went back to the house we were staying in; the workers had asked for more drinking water. The construction of the new house was progressing well. The roof was yet to be done, but the structure stood magnificent already. The house would be gigantic upon completion; it was the symbol of our father's hard work - years of sacrifice condensed into a fine piece of building to be remembered, by us- his family.

The masons were on the other side of the building as we played hide-and-seek in the unfinished rooms. They couldn't hear our giggles, not even our screams; they were busy with their songs and cigarettes.

My brother is two years older than me. He was my best friend till he started going out to play with his friends without taking me along. At home, with me, he gets bored very easily. And playing hide-and-seek in an unfinished house could entertain his young soul only for half an hour.

"I am bored, let's play something else!" he declared out of nowhere.

He wanted to play the detective game. He was a Sherlock fan. He was a brilliant student too: a rank holder.

Being taught to be forever obedient, I agreed to his plan as usual. We found a safety pin from the scrap, which served as the item to be detected upon someone hiding it. It was a small one; a bit rusted. It must have been one of Amma's lost pins.

I still wonder why she had to take us wherever she went. Her fear that something unpleasant may happen to us made her paranoid about leaving us alone at home. But that day, I wished she knew that danger lurked in places she thought were safe. I really wish that I wasn't there that day. For, any other form of danger would have been better.

So that day, as always, I was the first one to seek. And by some faint luck, I found the pin under a torn carpet. We played this for a while. One would stand with their eyes closed and the other went about hiding it. It was fun. And just when things started to get exciting, Amma came in with her usual announcement. "That's enough! Go eat the samosas they have brought. It's time for tea. I will be back in one hour. I need to buy something."

We nodded in agreement. And she nodded, accepting our agreement. Amma left.

It was my turn to find the pin. He had hidden it somewhere beyond my reach. I couldn't find it anywhere near the place he was standing. I looked for signs of movement. The bathroom door was moving. It meant that he had just gone inside it. And I rushed to the bathroom door, closed it behind me, and searched for that tiny piece of metal.

He also came running behind me, and stood near the door, watching me search my way to the safety pin's hiding place. The way he stood there calmed me a bit. But slowly, his eyes started to look alien to me. They weren't smiling at me. They saw something that they should have not seen while I kept searching for the pin uneasily. I checked for it in every brick hole, every small corner, and to reach the ventilation hole, I even hopped onto a stack of bricks beside me. I was desperate to find the pin and run out.

Him being near me never felt unusual to me. He has always been near. But this time, he didn't feel like the person I knew. He began touching me in a way he had never done before, and I suddenly didn't know what to do. No one had taught me how to stop my brother from clearing his doubts. All that I was taught was that we had to protect each other.

It is his marriage in a week and that too with the girl of his dreams. She is smart, fearless, adorable - everything packed into one. Neeta was everything he wanted, and every time he compares us, I scream within.

You shattered my faith in this world and now you think I am not living up to what is expected of me? What a joke!

His jokes strike me like stones and bring spittle to my mouth. He scarred me for life. And made me wonder about the meaning of family and love and everything of that sort.

I am twenty-one now, aware of abuse and of abusers, and maybe I would have healed from this trauma had it occurred just once. But this pain has become a part of me now. I can never sleep in a room that can't be locked from the inside. I cannot sleep on days when I am at home. And because of this fear, I began running away from my home with whatever money I could get. I still do.

I always wonder if I will ever be able to tell this to my mother. She thinks that my depression is a result of having an over-achieving brother and the fact that I couldn't rise up to his success. I think I will let her die believing that her son is the kindest person she knows. I guess, I would never tell her about the way he scarred a twelve-year-old girl, his only sister. I think pain has incapacitated me from inflicting pain of any sort upon anyone. Life is in fact very strange when it comes to how we survive calamities; we often become versions of ourselves that we never wished for. We tend to become people who we shouldn't be.

a brief encounter

Red, blue, green, and magenta. It was an odd combination of colours for a bangle set. But they seemed to suit her hands.

It was almost sunset and the sky was pouring down without a pause. It seemed that nature was crying over her losses – those irrevocable ones, the ones no one talks about. The rains were heavy this year. Perhaps the heaviest of what I have seen in three years. Kochi is still a bit unfamiliar to me. Her streets and the life that flows through her veins are a bit sophisticated. Maybe a bit too sophisticated for me to comprehend in three whole years of my life here.

This land, with its magical illusions, lures anyone who comes to her. Lit and unlit, there are many places here, where life goes on without much of a complaint. There is no silence here. It is often filled with suffocation and doubt. Doubts that make every breath heavy. And where I stand right now is one of them, lit with a street light that casts long shadows of shorter men. Without an umbrella to take me home, all I could do standing there was to observe the life around me. And I did.

She seemed unaware of the rains, and I guess, of all the world around. Lost in thought, her dark eyes reminded me of the old Bollywood actresses. She was beautiful, yet lifeless. There was a certain sadness in her smile – I could see that. The heavily decorated purple saree seemed a little misplaced for the weather, yet she seemed very comfortable in it. It was pouring down and people tried their best to put on the worst clothes they had. And there she was, dressed in the most charming way. Interesting, I felt.

She was standing right next to me and I could sense the smell of her perfume. Feminine. There were only three more people in the shade, taking refuge from the rain. They seemed to be highly occupied with the act of cursing the rain. And the rest of us, we were lost in our own thoughts.

It was a different feeling, observing a woman. I had never done that before. I felt a huge urge to talk to her, but I was afraid. And I felt funny at the thought of it. I was afraid if she would mistake me, or if she wouldn't like it. I felt nervous that the act may spoil this beautiful companionship I felt near her. I was being childish. Or crazy. I don't know.

"Where do you wanna go?" she asked.

Caught by surprise, I answered in an anxious tone, "Vypin."

She fell silent. Disappointed perhaps.

"What about you?"

"Mmm. Nowhere, I guess."

That was quite a strange answer, and I felt that she was making fun of me. But then I realized that it wasn't so. She wasn't anxious when the buses came near. Like us, she didn't check their boards eagerly.

Within a while, she started talking as if to a long-lost friend, and every time she asked me a question, I saw that her eyes sparkled. I saw a genuine curiosity in them.

She was glad that she made a friend. And I was glad she spoke to me. For the first time in my life, I felt someone was happy for me and I became fond of her immediately.

Natasha. That was her name; a name that I have never been able to forget after that brief encounter. With a gentle smile on her face, she asked me, "What about your family?"

"Well, no one like that I guess."

She looked confused at first, but then she smiled at me. I could see the kindness that filled in her eyes.

I asked her about her family. And she gave me an answer that confused me.

"Glad I have none either." And she smiled at that.

I was taken aback at first. How could someone ever say that? For me, my only wish in life is to have a family where I belong to. But something had made her feel that she was better off not belonging anywhere. And I felt weird about that. I didn't want to know the reason behind that thought of hers.

We both smiled at each other, awkwardly. Another bus passed by.

To distract myself from the awkwardness, I looked up at the sky. But the sky was barren. There were no stars today. They were hiding, I guess. Maybe they were smiling among themselves. Singing. Watching over the world and laughing at our hidden desires. And for a second I wished that she would take me as her family.

"What do you do?" Her voice startled me, bringing me back to the reality.

"I work as a teacher at The Earth School."

She returned a dull smile this time. And her hands reached for her bag, avoiding my face.

"You?"

She gave me a dull smile and said, "I sell my body."

I didn't know how to reply to that. I just looked at her as if I was hoping for an answer to a question that I never asked.

She lit a cigarette. She turned sideways and avoided my eyes.

I felt a huge urge to hug her, but the last bus to my hostel had already arrived by then. The rain had also stopped.

A water droplet sparkled on her red bhindi as I walked to that nearly empty bus to Vypin. We did not say our goodbyes.

das

I remember her laugh very clearly. And even more clearly, I remember the way she laughed- I could sense her jumping with joy. And for me, that was something new. She wasn't the kind of person I had seen before. Sorry, I didn't mean it literally. I can't see, but we do see people without our eyes, don't we? We see them in our heart. In a way. I am not sure how to put that across though!

I remember that she came to me, just to ask me if I was happy. And I didn't know what to say. That was the first time someone had asked me if I was happy. People like her rarely see people like me. We are invisible to most people actually. No one really cares about our existence until they see us dead. Even then, they take notice only because it is an inconvenience. Please don't think that I'm complaining about my life, I am not. I am rather okay with my life. I have a place to stay. I get three meals a day. I have a bunch of friends. In fact, I am content. My situation is better than how it used to be. But that day, when she asked me if I was happy, I suddenly felt empty.

For me, the absence of struggle was happiness. Having money to buy a meal was happiness. But I hadn't laughed as she did in ages. She seemed to be happy in a different way. And suddenly, the happiness I knew seemed like an empty shell. There was nothing in it that made me jump with joy. There was nothing in it that made me sing like she did- to sing out of the happiness one felt.

People call me Das. But my real name is Velu. I hail from a small village in the great Madurai district. I hail from a place where being born in a poor family often meant dying of hunger, and being the lucky person that I am, I was born blind too. No one knew why my parents left me with my grandmother and ran away. No one knows if they are still alive. When Paatti died, I knew I would soon be forced to leave the village. There were no jobs that I could do there. I had to survive. So, I packed my things and got on a bus to the town. I found a small job here; I collect money at the counter of a public toilet. I live a kilometre away from that. I live with my family; my wife and my daughter.

My little girl was born two weeks back. And today, when we brought her to our house and I held her in my arms, I remembered Tara. And finally, I understood what she meant that day. Finally, I felt happiness. And I wished that she was here to see me.

The thing with being accustomed to our lives is that we don't know what we miss until someone points it out to us. I often find it rather amusing.

The first time I felt this irony was when someone told me that I could have a family, that I could get married; to someone blind or otherwise. He told me there were people who were poorer than me. And that if I could provide someone with two meals a day, he could find someone to live with me. The thought that someone would marry me to save themselves from dying was strange. Nevertheless, it meant being loved, which was beautiful to think of. And until Kumar put this before me, I really didn't know that I wasn't being loved; I never felt the need either.

But what she pointed out that day wasn't about love. It wasn't about the business of life, the things we buy and sell on many layers. It was about what I was. She asked me if I had ever seen myself beyond the struggles. She asked me if I have ever felt life as a beautiful thing.

And my answer felt too heavy for myself. Because I hadn't. How could I?

I was poor. I was blind. And I had no one else in my life. I told her that a man cannot be happy for no reason. It was impossible.

I told her that for someone like her, happiness was an everyday thing. But for a person like me, happiness is a story we tell ourselves to keep living through another day.

And she laughed.

"Here Das, you didn't say a word about you other than your struggles. Now think again. Think as a human being, not as a pile of tragedies."

She asked me to remember the last time I was happy.

And I couldn't speak for a while.

Suddenly my Paatti's[4] voice rang in my ears. The clamour of the people around and the blaring sounds of the road fell silent. I could hear her gentle giggles. I could hear her shouting at the chicken that ate her seeds.

I suddenly felt her wrinkled skin as they hugged me. I felt the coldness of her face the last time I touched her. The memories of holding her hands to cross the road flooded my being. I felt the hot wind brush against my cheeks as we walked for hours to fetch our ration. For a second, my village throbbed in me. I felt the dampness of the earth, after a monsoon shower, beneath my feet and tears rushed down my cheeks.

The next thing I knew was Tara hugging me.

She hugged me with a deep sigh.

She didn't ask me what. She just told me that happiness should never be in our memories alone.

She walked with me to my house that day. I asked her why she was here, and she told me that she was on a pilgrimage. It was strange for a young girl of her age to be on a pilgrimage, but then, unlike others, she wasn't searching for some Gods. She didn't have to.

---

[4] Paatti refers to grandmother, or someone as old.

She told me that she would come and see me whenever she comes to Madurai.

But I have never again heard her voice.

She never returned to see me. And somehow, a part of me knew about it that day itself.

For some people are meant to be a part of our life only for a brief period of time. They leave us when they complete their part in our story. They ought to, or we would get stuck to them just the way we get stuck to everything that makes us forget our pain. But these people who leave sooner than the others are the people who stay with us the longest. They leave a part of them within us, forever.

A part of Tara stays on with me. It will, always.

She made me see that I wasn't my struggles. She took away the weight that I had been carrying on my shoulders. And in its place, she left behind a bit of happiness that she was. She reminded me that life existed beyond the tangible.

Maybe that is why I don't remember Tara as a person; I can only remember her as light.

the indian coffee house

It looked as though it would rain in a few seconds. The clouds were dark; swollen with water. The earth looked grey; everything began to move at a slow pace. The clouds hid the sun but the heat kept building up. The air began to feel heavy, and slowly everything stood still. The breath was held, the hands were frozen and eyes refused to blink. But my ears were sharpened, tuned to hear just one voice. And my heart; that poor little thing, I think it stopped.

"I am not sure of the risk I am taking Lachu. But somehow I feel that I shouldn't stop myself from saying this now."

I took one short breath. My eyes blinked, I guess.

"I am not the kind of guy with whom you can chill out with; I wouldn't crack jokes in public, I often find the silent spaces more comfortable. I am not a very cool person either. I talk about politics. And I guess I am into so much of it that I rarely get time for myself, to be honest. And a person like you might have a lot of dreams that are way beyond my thoughts or the way I live. I don't want to spoil them."

The clouds looked darker now, the air- denser; suffocating maybe! I could feel my lungs struggling.

"But listen! I have always, that is, from the first time we spoke till this moment, I have loved you. And for the first time in life, I am taking the risk, to express what I feel to someone I have known for a short while."

I looked up at the ceiling. There were cobwebs. I smiled at them.

I have always wondered at the magic the universe brings into our lives. Sometimes it is beyond human expectations, and often, beyond human comprehension. I couldn't help but smile.

For me, the clouds suddenly vanished. And my eyes shut close for a few seconds in prayer. Two years of waiting! Two years of smiling at the ceiling. Two long years of not saying a word, answered now in the most beautiful way. '*I have always loved you*'.

-

He stood up to greet us. He had a very soft smile and a very soft look! It really amused me, the difference in the ways between our Chairperson and him, the Chairman of the College Union, Government Law College, Ernakulam. Our first meeting was hardly a few minutes of smiling before the waiter returned the balance. But for the first time in my life, I felt fond of a place that I usually didn't like. For the first time, the Indian Coffee House felt warm.

"Jaya, I think Lachu has got a wide smile here! I smell a crush!" Though I recognized Munnu's gleaming face, I was too lost in thoughts to acknowledge her and as usual, pick up a fight. That man didn't impress me, he rather reminded me of a lost generation of kind people and that was very special for me.

I have always found it hard to handle the excitement. Somehow my voice just gives in.

And a call from your crush is more than exciting when all that you have done in a weeks' time is to talk about him. I still remember how they were making fun of him as he spoke to me and I recall very fondly the word he used to describe what they were doing to him. 'Thejovadahm'. And I am glad that I didn't know the meaning of that word as it became the reason for us to continue talking.

-

Months rolled by. We would meet in between. Not often, but still a few times in a month. We would smile at each other and say nothing, while our friends stood around and arranged our democratic system in the most proper manner.

Almost all the time, I fell in love with the strength of his soul and the beauty of his ethics. He never assumed a space, but everyone respected the greatness he tried to hide. The fire in his eyes when he spoke about something that was important to him would be enough to move a crowd into action. He was a powerful orator. He wasn't the so-called handsome, well-built guy that I normally got a crush on. He was an ordinary, loose shirt, no watch, poem type of person. But that difference made all the difference in the world; it made him even dearer.

Slowly, but steadily, I grew very fond of him. He became a friend. He became a reminder that there will be a place that I can call home when my parents are no more. For me, he became the strength that pushed me through everything that came my way. We spoke more in silence than words, but we knew that we were heard and understood. And that was more than beautiful.

-

Today, as I note this down, he is reading in the small library that we have at home. Not once has he asked me what I scribble so much, which I do a lot. Rather he would peep in, hug me from behind and ask in the softest voice I have ever heard, "Would you mind me taking a look?" And that modest question often defeats my fear of being judged. In his hands, every word of mine stays safe; read without bias, read without judgment. That is the most I could ever ask for- a place that feels safe, a person that is home. And now when I recall, I often thank Toolika for deciding on the Indian Coffee House that day.

a conversation I overheard

"Shiv, has someone close to you ever died?" Meera asked.

"No."

"I guess that's why we keep fighting."

Shiv could not comprehend that. It was beyond his reasoning mind to understand how death could mean something so important to another person. How it could change their life. Death to him was a reality upon which all life rested. And he never understood how someone could not accept it.

"It's not that I don't accept death. It's just that when you look at life from that side of the mirror, everything looks completely strange. Everything seems to be absurd. Yet all the more meaningful. It's just that once we know what death does to the life that we live, something in us begins to become both greedy and nihilistic at the same time."

"Maybe you are overthinking it Meera. Maybe you need to see that pain is there in all of us. That some of us choose to handle it differently."

"Hmm, yes. The problem is with handling. The problem is with handling the fear of death that takes away all the dear ones, of not being able to see them again. Even when you walk out to get your bus to college. Even when you walk away into the kitchen. It's a plague that takes your life away.

I have been trying to normalize death; to make myself believe in the eventuality of it. But every time I do, I come across questions that weren't there the last time."

"Isn't it too selfish of you Meera? This fear is only about you, about you having to feel lonely or you losing or you suffering damage. Why don't you see that everyone goes through this?"

"It is selfish, but then, this is how I feel. It's not just the loss that scares me. The silence that follows death. The uncertainty. The inability to know life as we know it now. The idea that we can never talk again. Never feel. Never know the warmth of another life. It's all just too scary for me. It makes me feel exhausted. The very act of living itself seems absurd then."

"But Meera, being sad makes the existing absurd life more absurd, doesn't it?"

"Yeah. I know. And it is only because I know that part that I insist on happiness more than ever. That's exactly why I keep telling you we should hug more often. Kiss more often. To hold each other's hands more often. And that's exactly why I also tell you that it makes me cry when I say an unkind word to my mom.

I just know that this life, this moment here, is too precious since we do not know anything beyond this. And the absurdity of it all gives a meaning to it that is too profound for our logic to grasp."

"Maybe you should stop reading all this philosophy, Meera. It's screwing with your head."

"I guess it helps. At least I know I am not alone."

"You were crying just now and now you are smiling. I don't understand. What is this?"

"I guess, I'm just too greedy for life. I feel it all together, all at once. And that leaves me struggling."

"What should I do then?"

"You can maybe hug me. And remind me that you are there for me, that I am being loved despite everything."

"...."

bhakthi

She was in her thirties. I am not sure of her exact age and I guess it is of no relevance to this story.

Her days would begin really early. Before the sun rays kissed the plants in her small garden, her gentle hands would touch them, and the chants she recited would course through their veins, waking them up for the day. There would be flowers in her garden, always. Her Gods, the ones that live in her small pooja room, were never without the floral extravaganza. Her house would fill with the scent of the flowers and the mild fragrance from the incense she burns.

She walks barefoot most of the time. The soles of her feet were always coloured by the earth, and her palms were coloured yellow from the turmeric and vermillion. She always wore a strange lightness on her face, something that I knew came from the very same reason why she walks barefoot.

I don't normally pay much attention to the people around. But some people are actually worth spending our time on. Some people remind us of the things we otherwise forget or never really come to face within ourselves. She reminds me of love. She reminds of love as I might have known before I learned the word.

And that is why I thought I should tell you about this woman who lives next door. About Kamala akka[5].

Dr. Kamaleswari Kumar is a professor in Gender Studies at the University of Puducherry. Her students have the freedom to call her Kamala and to talk to her about anything and everything that concerns their studies and their personal lives. She is a wonderful teacher and a very warm person. As an academician, the clarity with which she talks might be too much for those who lack passion; but beyond that personality, there is an aspect of her that no one can clearly articulate, something that puts a smile on your face without your clear understanding. That part of her lights up something in us. And I am glad it does.

The last time I met someone who belonged to this kind of people, I began questioning the very foundations on which my life was built: career, wealth, social status; everything seemed too absurd to me then.

Amarnath lived in a realm that was beyond these insignificant parades. He lived in a realm where he had become light. And the first person I spoke to after meeting Kamala akka was him. I knew Amar would understand her. I knew that he would tell me how it was possible for someone to live an entire life saying that Lord Shiva was her lover and spend her evenings

---

[5] Akka refers to an elder sister, or someone older than oneself.

offering flowers to a roadside shrine, telling the world that she has come to spend some time with her dear one. And Amar did tell me how it was possible, and that in bhakthi[6], one transcends all the dualities we know of. Dualities of life and death, of right and wrong, of the logical and the illogical- everything burns up. Sanity and insanity are for the minds that haven't touched the core of themselves- that which is within, that which permeates all that is and all that isn't. He told me that I should learn to simply be with her and not try to understand her.

---

[6] Bhakthi refers to devotion.

And he was right. To understand her was impossible. Her clear-cut logic takes a side seat moments before she collects Chempak flowers for her lover. From then, it is just her, her love and her love that encompasses the whole of this existence. She would be drunk on life by the time the evening light fades. And then, in a soft melodious voice, she would chant some verses, and then move on to chores of the otherwise mundane life. Watching her in these brief moments, in these moments of absolute devotion that she lived by, has touched my being in a way I can never fully explain. What Amar unsettled in me was settled by her with great ease. Not a word was spoken between us, but after those evenings in her presence, it no longer mattered what happened around me; the absurd and the meaningful, both lost its charm to affect me. She brought to me a smile that came from an acceptance toward life; a smile that came from knowing love a little differently.

These days, I don't spend time watching her. We do go and collect Chempak flowers together whenever possible and eat samosas from the street vendor, watching the tides. We smile at each other when we meet at college. And I guess that is enough.

return

It rained heavily that day. There wasn't any sign of human life; the roads were empty, the streets dull. The earth, filled with water, leaked and filled the potholes with orange liquid. The patches of tarred road glistened; the rain made them look anew. The smell of the earth, particularly of the rotting leaves, made it feel that the world was growing tired of the downpour. It had been over a week now, everything yearned for a bit of sunlight.

The earth wasn't green anymore; it was grey. Rarely do people from the outside understand when I say this, but for people like us, who have lived all their lives in the hills know what I mean when I say that the earth becomes grey. It is one of the unusual realities of our lives. When it rains in December, the mist thickens and covers the place almost entirely. It becomes difficult to see the other person even if they are just a metre away. The clouds above add to the menace as well. In fact, it is that time of the year when the sun-deprived lives shut themselves in tiny rooms, candle-lit and warm. But for me, this season brings joy. It is the winters that let me go out without seeing too many faces.

My father was from Kottayam: Abraham Tharakan,

a post-graduate in English Literature from the legendary CMS College. He found himself working as an Estate Manager at the age of twenty-three. He settled in the hills with his family. My mother, Annie Abraham, came from a wealthy family in Vypin. She was an orthodox Catholic, a pious, strict, and strong woman. Appa had lost his father long back, even before he married my mother, and being the youngest son, his mother, Lillykutty (my dearest grandmother), came to live with us. It meant hours of applying oils to relieve her rheumatic pains, but nevertheless, she made the coldness of this place a bit more bearable back then. She had a way of her own.

It was in the year 1982 that I was born. Back then, Kuttikkanam had nothing but few tea shops and lots of mist. I was born on the night before Christmas. It was cold. In Appa's words, it was freezing cold. Amma gave birth to me without much struggle, she was a very healthy woman, and being raised by her, I grew up into a woman who could disagree with her and make my own choices. It has been a year since she left me, but her uncompromising attitude lurks everywhere in this house. Eldo, who takes care of the garden, still maintains the space the way she'd liked it. Ammini chechi still cooks the way my mother used to prefer it. In fact, this house was about my father's stories and her stubbornness. And I grew up, all about the way my grandmother reflected on my parent's life. She often found them funny.

After Appa passed away, Amma rarely bothered

about how happy we were. I was only sixteen then, I needed her; but she refused me a space in her heart. She closed it on all human beings and opened it to the invisible Gods, and the people who spoke about the miracles of those Gods. Around that time, it was my grandmother who taught me how to find home in myself. She taught me how to make the perfect black coffee, how to make fire and how to make the perfect omelette. She made me learn how to drive the jeep as well. In my mother's absence, she instilled in me a certain kind of courage that comes with age alone. She made me look at life lightly, on the insignificance of many things. She also taught me how to love.

Coming back to the winters, I love the way everything seems to go almost still at this time of the year. It might be an outcome of living alone all these years, but I have come to like minimal human interactions. I no longer like to explain why I haven't married, or how I manage to live alone. I also hate explaining how I don't feel lonely. But today, I am excited about meeting a few people. I am so excited that I am wearing a saree after a decade or so. After about seventeen years, the man I once loved is coming home. His daughters too. In fact, I am more excited to see them. Rahel and Rebecca.

Coming back to the winters, another thing that I like about this season is the way sometimes, just sometimes, the way sunlight peeps in through the mist to touch our beings. To stand there, basking in the light and the warmth of that ray of sunlight; it often reminds me what hope feels like. Hope is like sunlight when the soul grows heavy; sunlight, when we least expect it. And today, the hope of happiness fills my veins. Like Amma's old wine, it rushes through my being, colouring my cheeks red.

The thing about memories is that they uproot the walls that we build around us in a matter of seconds. Nihaal's call sent me back to those dimly lit corridors of our college, to the tea at Bhaskar's, to the long walks back home, and the pine trees that still remember the way we kissed. Falling in love with him was almost natural for me back then, we grew up together and our worlds were almost the same. His father worked in the estate nearby- our homes were just a minute's walk apart. We read books, fought over my grandmother's *elayappam*[7], and argued over who spoke better English.

It was not my father who had a problem with our relationship, it was my mom who refused her daughter to be sent into a family of Tamil Hindus. Her face not only showed disapproval but also showed disgust. Back then, her opposition didn't mean much to me, but it did affect him. We graduated with fairly good scores, each moved into a different city and lost what I had fought for. It did hurt me, the way he vanished from my life without a word. But I was raised to be a strong woman; I couldn't break, I

---

[7] elayappam- a snack made from rice flour with sweet filling inside.

wouldn't. I went on to pursue my life, its colours, and all that it could offer. It is only when I lost Amma that Kuttikkanam came back into my life; now I had to find answers to tell others and I had to make peace with my mother. But first, I had to make peace with myself.

All that we indulge in, to forget the pain that runs deep within, fails at some point or the other. Now mortality stared at me in the face. And the absence of love felt more painful than ever. And that is when life began to look strange to me.

Nihaal found out that I was back home. Antony, our classmate, was back in town for a visit and he had told him that I was here, taking care of the estate. We started talking a month back. I didn't want to know why he left, that was understandable. I wanted to know what he did with his life afterwards.

He did well actually. He now works with a leading magazine. He has become the chief editor. He has two daughters, twins. They lost their mother to cancer two years before. Now four, they are being taken care of by his mother, my dear Lalitha aunty. My heart swelled at the thought of seeing her again. The last time I saw her was at my father's funeral. She held me all the while, till they buried him, not my mother.

It was me who asked him to come home. I wanted to see him. I wanted to see the girls. If possible, I wanted to go back with him to see Lalitha aunty. I was excited and too full of love. After a certain age, love redefines itself. In your thirties, lust doesn't burn the cells as it does in the twenties, and that means you become less compulsive. You become more like a character in a novel written by Tolstoy; you act out of your love that has matured. It wants happiness for others too.

The car has arrived finally. Poor heart, it just wants to run to the door and see them. But I walk out of my room, gently, and open the door to watch the little ones plucking my mother's favourite petunias and throwing them all over the place. Nihaal smiles. I couldn't help but laugh. Those were my mother's favourite ones. Look at the way love returns!

grief

I tend to think a lot about death these days. To be honest, that is all that I think about. But I rarely share these thoughts with anyone. I don't know if Anand would want to know them. I don't think he approves of these contemplations on death. After all, I am expected to be happy and strong before Nila. She needs a mother to whom she can run to, no matter what.

Amma was the most important person in my life. I don't think there is anything I wouldn't do to have her back, to be near her and to have her presence when I get back home. I would do anything to lay down on her lap when the world wears me out.

But now that I don't have her and that I can't cry, I am filled with the same old thoughts about death. Where do people go after death?

Can they hear us?

Or see us?

Are they alone there?

Or does a place like that even exist? A realm where we go after the body is left behind?

I really don't know.

On some days, the milk spills out of the pan, reminding me about the life ahead; the life I am expected to live. On other days, Anand hugs me from behind, when the vastness of the blue sky engulfs me. Sometimes I think that gravity alone couldn't have held me down to the planet. If it wasn't for him, I would have left a long time ago. These are the few moments when I distract myself from the loop I have gotten myself into. I find peace in distractions these days.

How humans adapt at the face of calamities is strange.

Nila keeps asking me why I stopped drinking coffee. How I do tell her that I remove those things that I love the most about my life upon losing the people I shared that joy with. She would never know why I stopped making plans about a world tour. Why I no longer wear Kolhapuri sandals. She would never recognise her mother who loved train journeys; the only Amrutha she knows is one who loves her father's SUV and their weekend trips to Kumily.

Oh, I am sorry. I lost track again. I was telling you about my thoughts on death.

I lost someone I dearly loved early in my life. But I lived through it. It didn't destroy me beyond damage. But it changed the way I perceive life. I was able to see life from the vantage point of death. Life oscillated between being absurd and being divinely profound. It split me into two, and now, after losing Amma, the duality is over. It is sheer emptiness. Life stands still with a deadly silence that comes from unsettled chaos.

The love I sought might have healed me. But I grew tired of searching for it in people and places. Maybe it's non-existent. Perhaps, it's a hope that is only meant to keep me alive. On some days, I look at Nila and I find that love within me. Though it is directed outward, it settles me for a while. A part of me recognises that love in Anand, but I guess I don't have the energy to accept it anymore. I am struggling with this emptiness in my heart and I feel that there is no way out. On most days, I am very tired; I don't think I have the strength to hold on to this pain anymore.

Amma always used to say that love is the only thing that can cheat death. And in her case, she was absolutely right. Until I die, her love will have cheated death brilliantly. But then, it always makes me wonder if anyone would ever find such a love that lasts a lifetime. A child, as long as their mothers live, basks in that love. What about afterwards? Where do they go with that emptiness they suddenly feel? What can fill them, what can take the place of that love? And then, in those junctures, I remind myself that death is perhaps the kindest of all things in the larger scape of reality. I cannot do anything more, can I?

pauli

The truth is, life is the best thing that can happen to us. No matter how hard it is, this chance to be alive is the greatest blessing one can ask for. But the saddest part is that you will realise this only when death stares at you in the face.

I always thought I would live a better life in some distant future with the girl I love. But the future is just a hope. We must invest in the life that we have at hand. In my case, I should have made peace with my father. With his stubbornness. And with my mother, for her passivity. But it never happened and I don't think it can happen before I die. And that hurts me. I now wish I had loved everyone and everything a bit more passionately. I regret saving love for the sake of convenience and for the sake of not looking foolish before a society that thought love was just another emotion. How I wish that people knew what death was, just so that they realise that love is all that is.

I always thought that I had time. And now I know that it was one big lie.

We call him Pauli. His father named him Paulson. Paulson Philip. His father was a very popular public figure; a sworn atheist, rationalist, and environmentalist. I cannot think of that man without a grudge. No one else had a heart as cold as his.

Pauli died of cancer. There was a growth in his brain, the tumour was diagnosed a month before Sharika got her job in the Forest Department. Their plan was to get married immediately after they both got a job.

Pauli was quite a reckless person. He lived his life on his terms, that too, often at odds with his father's plans. But a part of him that I can never forget was the way he treasured the relationship with his friends. He held them higher than most things in his life. He used to call us family and he always meant that.

His death hasn't yet settled in me. Unlike the death of any other person in your life, the death of a dear friend can completely alter the way you live. There is a vacuum that feels irreplaceable and it is. The pain of losing a friend is not sharp, but it hurts you longer. Every time I light a cigarette, my eyes search for him. Every time I start my bike, I have to steer myself away from the route where he lived. I have no one else to see there, not anymore.

Pauli and Sharu were in love. They fell in love back when we were in school. She was our junior. Her mother passed away when she was in high school. And a year ago, her father left her as well. It was then that they decided to get married as soon as possible. Their love was a beautiful thing to watch. They were in love just like two plants that grow together. They gave each other space but held each other from falling. They sang their favourite songs when they walked their way back home. We would make fun of their attachment. But today, all I know is that without her, Pauli would have given up much sooner.

The last time I met him was on his birthday. Of all the things he told me, one thing remains unsettled; unforgotten. He talked about time. He talked about the transience of time.

Everything we hold on to must be left behind one day, and all that time leaves for us to take with us, is love.

Tell Sharu that our love was the only meaningful thing that happened to me.

His voice quivered at this. And I remember how he gasped.

His voice remains in my head.

Pauli asked me to wait. It felt as if he wanted to tell me a lot of things. As if he was aware that he had very little time before him. He was in a hurry, he wanted to share all that he carried within.

Remember that day I told you about going to the doctor? I had asked my father to call a taxi, by then I could barely read anything on the boards. But he told me that I must go by bus. He said that I must not spend unnecessarily. And he also said that I must be back before night so that the rice would not be wasted.

He smiled. He looked up at the ceiling and stared.

And within me, anger filled up like anything.

The day he was talking about was very vivid in my memory. I accompanied him to the doctor that day. His weak body leaning against mine, he sat there in absolute silence. He was in pain, both physical and mental. But I didn't know that his father had said something like this. His father knew about the tumour. He just didn't care.

For some reason, after Pauli's death and all that happened along with it, I value my family a lot more than I used to. My mother, who comes running with this concoction or the other upon the slightest hint of fever in me, felt surreal to me. The world is a strange place.

It is true that as death comes closer, we regret the love we didn't give. But when it stands really closer, it becomes all the more difficult to leave the people we dearly loved. And then, love becomes the most painful thing. I want you to see to it that Sharu gets married. Once her sister is married off, she'll have no one else. I don't want that to happen to her.

Koshi, I want you to know that I would have died rotten, if it wasn't for her. When my parents felt repulsed by the stench of shit and urine, they called her in to take care of me. My idealist father said that marriage was just a social custom. She stayed with me despite all the disagreements from her family. This father of mine once told me that she comes from a lower-class family and that there is no benefit in marrying her. I wonder if she would have stayed in this house for a second if she knew their intentions.

Pauli sighed. His hands were trembling. I could see his eyes filling up.

On one of those days, when my father told her that she has to pay for her meals, I wished for my death. And I was glad that she didn't have to put up with them by marrying me. For a second there, I was glad that I was going to die.

I asked her to leave.

His voice began to break again.

Before he began another sentence, his father called him from the living room. He asked if Pauli had made the call yet. I eyed him, asking which call it was.

Pauli smiled and asked me to get his mobile. He asked me to dial Raghavan. And I did.

But what I heard after Raghavan picked up the call froze my heart.

Raghava, why aren't your men here yet? If it starts raining, it is going to be difficult to dig the pit. Father wants it ready by tomorrow. Please make it fast. You know how angry he can get.

I could hear Raghavan say yes.

Pauli smiled again.

He didn't know that he would die in another three days, but a part of me wished that he died the earliest.

His father's voice still rings in my ears. Those words make my chest ache.

"Will they come tomorrow? It looks like it will start raining soon."

Pauli died just before the monsoon hit the land. The sky wept only after his father buried his body.

freedom

"Rosamme, did you wash the kennel?"

"*Aamm!*" I yelled from the cowshed.

"Rosamme, can you fetch the oil for me?"

"I will be there in a second Ammachi, let me finish cleaning the shed."

"Alright! Just make it fast. The bride's family will arrive in two hours."

I suppose you imagined an old lady, waiting helplessly for someone. Or perhaps a kind, graceful grandmother, nearing her final days, excited about her son's wedding. I'm afraid she's neither of those things. She is what some people would call 'notorious'. You wouldn't want to meet a woman like her and I'll tell you why.

By the way, my name is Rosakutty; "kutty" in Malayalam means "small child". But I am not a child. I am twenty-three years old. And a mother to a three - year-old, autistic boy.

My parents were killed in a landslide. Their bodies were never found. They were quite loving, especially my mother. They were working at Ammachi's cardamom plantation when they got trapped in the landslide. It was July, the peak of monsoon and landslides are common during the monsoon here; one fine day, an entire region might get washed away. Everything would be gone, and only dirt and ruins would remain. Lives would become tales in a matter of seconds.

Since my parents died in a very common scenario, not everyone showed sympathy to us. My brother got married a month after my parents died. The excuse was to have someone to take care of me. But he left the village in another two weeks. He married a woman he met at the brothel. She was a beautiful girl and he fell in love with her. He told me that in order to live peacefully with the love of his life, he had to leave this village. He had to find a place where no one knew her. And I couldn't stop him. I just wished them luck and waited by the door every day. I knew that one predator or the other would turn up to 'save' me.

I do have my mother's parents living somewhere in Tamil Nadu. But I didn't think it was right to burden them, so I never went to them. As I had hoped, Ammachi had come to rescue me the moment she heard about my brother's marriage. She told me that she would give me a place to stay and food, and some money for other essentials. She knew that her offer would buy me in and she was right, what she offered was enough for me. It felt better to not feel like an orphan. It felt better to think that I wouldn't have to sleep hungry.

Karikkattil House was a scary place in itself; an old mansion amidst eighty acres of cardamom plantation. The place was built during the colonial period. It held in it a strange sense of anger and submission. The earth upon which it stood had many lives buried underneath – mostly children, who were fathered by men who didn't know which women they took to bed.

Ammachi ruled the house, its men, and its dogs. There were three men and seven dogs. All of them were giants. There were other women in the house who were not Ammachi. But they were objects to be looked at, had sex with, and when Ammachi deems right, were supposed to bring forth another generation.

I wasn't allowed to talk to those women. Ammachi knew I had nothing to lose and that it made me fearless. Ammachi worried that I would pollute the submissive minds of her daughters-in-law.

Ammachi always wore a white Chatta and Mundu. She clads herself in the most pious ways. Very little gold. Very little luxury. She was very old and equally vicious. I still don't understand how someone can believe that they had the authority to hurt others and keep them their slaves forever. She walked with a power that made you stammer before her. I don't understand that kind of madness.

Her husband retired as a manager from the Karadigudi estate. He was British in his spirit. There was a portrait of him in the hallway. He had wicked eyes. I was thankful that he died long ago. The house had enough cruelty without him. He left behind a huge fortune and this woman had held it in her hands in a way he would have been proud of.

I often remember my mother as I sit by the fire in this house. During the first few months of being in this place, I regretted not getting married when my mother was alive. But then something told me that I had to live. That staying alive was important. And for that, I had to listen to Ammachi. I must let her sons sleep with me. I must let strangers grab my breasts. I must work until my bones hurt. And I must never complain. If I did, Ammachi would bury me just like she buried Anto's first wife.

We don't think of our self-worth when it comes to existing. In the third month of being in that house, I knew that I had another life growing within me. And I bore it, despite Ammachi's efforts to abort it. I fought for that life, and I won.

I gave birth to him on the day before Christmas. It was freezing cold, but that small piece of life in my hands made my heart feel warm. I felt hope seeping into my being. Life was finally worth the struggle.

But Ammachi made sure that this child would not live in her house.

She threatened Anto, who was thirty-six by then, that she would write half of his property for the child if he didn't put him in an orphanage. You can guess what Anto would have done.

My boy is three years old now. I see him every Sunday after the holy mass. I don't take him in my arms. I don't go near him. I am afraid I would want him beside me. In order to avoid pain, I stay afar and smile. I don't know if he recognises me, but he smiles. The priest who is in charge of the orphanage tells me that my little boy has learned to paint. What a joy for a mother to see her child grow! But who knew the pain of a mother forced to see her child grow an orphan, in the cold rooms of a charity home?

Today is his father Anto's engagement. Ammachi made sure that the house was impeccably clean. She made it a point that all the children and the women were silent when the guests would be at home. She was waiting at the storeroom for me to oil her leg and then take a bath. She was in a hurry to get ready before the strangers arrived.

I could see her rather frustrated figure from the cowshed. I washed off the traces of cow dung from my hands and picked up the knife Anto had bought for me.

I want to tell you a story that my mother once told me before I tell you what happened. It's about freedom. About Gandhi, who went to jail as a part of his fight for the freedom of this country. She used to get goosebumps every time she narrated it. The moral of her story was obvious: she wanted to raise me as a woman who could endure all things. But my point here is something else. Gandhi risked his life for freedom. And that is not a small thing. Because I know what it takes to do that.

Passivity has a threshold. Human beings can bend only so far. I just want you to know that.

I killed her that day. Anto had bought me the finest knife. One stab and she gasped for air. She did try to hit me, but her body couldn't agree with her. It was old. It didn't fight. Her seventy-two-year-old body fell dead in my arms while the whole family was busy getting ready for the guests. Maybe they knew it; that someone would kill her. No one in that house would grieve her loss. They had enough of her madness.

Anto had arranged for a Jeep for me to leave. And he had informed the priest that I would come to take my child back. The jeep dropped us off at the bus stand. The old man smiled at me. I think he knew.

I walked all the way to the Kumily check post, with my child on my waist. He was seeing the outside world for the first time. He was excited. So was I. I smiled at all the people who noticed us. We searched for a place to go. We picked a bus that had a movie playing in it. It would take us to Rameshwaram.

My mother had always wanted to go to Rameshwaram. She used to say that one will find salvation at that shore. Maybe she is right. That very thought made me smile. Anto promised me that the police would not come looking for me. He told me that they never came looking for him when he killed his wife because Ammachi wanted her killed.

The cold air brushed my cheeks. I smiled at the child sleeping on my chest. I was free, and it felt good.

vasanthi

Estate bungalows are a world in themselves. They are those tiny holes on the planet through which one can fall and be forgotten forever. They have their rules, their own ways of functioning. I was always scared of their cold insides; the stone walls and the spine-chilling silence they bred. The Planter's Bungalow, which was right before my house, was a place that I had never dared to step in. Until he asked me to. He was an old man with a rifle and he had a mad son.

We call him Mathew Sir. His wife died recently; no one knows the reason though. Some even say that he killed her. But I don't want to believe these stories.

I am seventeen years old. My name is Vasanthi. This is the third estate my parents are working in. The earlier one had a manager who wouldn't let us sleep in peace. He had wicked eyes on my mother and by the time we left, he had his eyes on me. But Mathew sir was kind to us. He heard our story and told us to stay in the lanes near the bungalow. He promised us safety. But the lady's death seems to have turned him cold. He doesn't smile that often these days. I don't know if he would go mad too.

His mad son was always silent. His silence was the

scariest part of him. His dark eyes were frozen. His gaze, steady. His sullen face had marks of torture upon them, but no one knew who tortured him. He refused to wake up the day they buried his mother. He never cried.

Like I said before, I had never been to the bungalow until he asked me to come in that day. My mother was right outside the building and I had nothing to worry about. I went in slowly. I could hear my heartbeat. But what awaited me was something I had never imagined. It wasn't a threat. It wasn't the scary silence of a mansion. Rather, it was a giggle; of a small life covered in wool. It wasn't important for me who its parents were. It was awake, asking me to lift it up. I picked up the child and I looked at the old man. His head was low. He was thinking, I guess.

As we both walked out, me with the child in my arms, he asked my mother if it was okay for her to take care of this child. Suddenly, he rephrased and asked if she would allow me to take care of the child. Confused, my mother nodded.

And I called her Ammu. She became mine.

I still do not know if the old man was her father or his mad son, or if she is an orphan that reached his doorsteps somehow. The old man wasn't fond of her anyway. He hated her fragile body and her loud cries. He was annoyed by her. It wasn't much of a surprise to me, but what did surprise me was my mother's behaviour. My mother, whom I never thought could be gentle, taught me how to feed her and how to put her to sleep. She taught me how to hold her comfortably. Soon Ammu became my child and me, her mother. I became someone's home so suddenly that it almost felt surreal.

I still wonder how my mother loves me. I have always felt like an intruder in her eternal struggle of managing our livelihood, but now, after Ammu, I can imagine her as having dearly held me. As having fed me, as having sung songs to put me to sleep, as excited at my baby steps, as having cleaned my poop with a smile. I can now think of her, as smiling at me. And I am beginning to experience life as a bit more joyful thing. The change a single life can bring is astonishing, isn't it?

The bungalow no longer scares me. Neither its cold insides nor the mad man's stares. Her meaningless giggles and her threatening cries are enough to keep our souls warm. She keeps us all on our toes but she warmed up that cold building just the way she warmed up three human hearts. I often find myself in gratitude for that.

There is a Gulmohar tree right outside the bungalow. The tree is a sight in itself. Older than most of us here, the tree has lived through a lot. It has been a witness to much. It has seen life and it has seen many deaths. It has seen lives that are as good as dead also. The mighty tree has also seen many revolutions. And it has seen bloodshed for the sake of power. It has seen love. And it has seen loss. The tree has a sense of power about it that comes with age. Something that has an effect on anyone who takes a look at her.

The Gulmohar flowers fall on the earth, making it look as if the earth was bleeding afresh from a long-forgotten scar. The flowers then wait to become the earth and they eventually do, without worrying about losing themselves.

Ammu loves the tree. She is three now. Her pet squirrel pays her a visit every morning. She rarely felt hungry while playing with the little guy. Her giggles make me want to run with her and play, but my mother thinks that it is inappropriate for me to play with her at my age. I give in.

My mother is worried about the whole situation. About my fiancé finding out about the child and misunderstanding it. According to Paati, my grandmother, raising this child itself is a big setback in the marriage market. Since I was raised to believe that the best thing I could do with life is to be a marriage-worthy woman, I didn't know if I could say something against her opinion.

The weight of our life often sits very heavily upon my shoulders. The fact that happiness is a rare entity is something that often worries me. Things have come to a place where happiness makes me wonder if something is wrong.

My mother smells of cardamom dust. No, not the sweet smell of cardamom, but the pungent smell that comes from handling dried cardamom and sorting them. My father smells of the earth and sweat. He reminds me of survival, of the definite end, and of the only future, while my mother reminds me of all the struggles in between. They raised me because it was expected of them. They were always tired. I have never seen them happy except when they went back to our homeland for the Thiruvizha[8]. I have seen my mother's eyes sparkle with the joy of meeting her dear ones. I have heard my father laugh with his friends. But here, like the earth we stood upon, they were cold. The mist seemed to have seeped into their beings, freezing the emotion of joy.

My parents were always frustrated. They were beaten down by the unfairness of life; of having to wake up at three in the morning and work till they were sore and still being in debt. I guess, we would all be frustrated in that case. They are tired of never getting to wear good clothes. They are tired of having nothing to hold on to but poverty. Their biggest dream is to own a decent mattress. To wake up without aches and marks on their skin. They hope to own a warm blanket someday after they marry me off, after they settle their debts. Sometimes I feel sad that

---

[8] Thiruvizha refers to a village carnival that is often associated with a temple.

the Gods didn't even bless them with a boy, and I feel sad that I would never be able to take care of them without a stranger letting me do that.

I do not know if I sympathise with my parents anymore or if I sympathise with my own life for that matter. I have come to accept this as my life. I have come to believe that this is what is meant for us. My life has taught me this one thing very clearly: the struggles of the body are far more bearable than the struggles of the mind. If a man is not to suffer either, then he should be like Swami.

Swami never spoke a word but Shiva. He would always be found near the temple, or sitting near the Gulmohar, or lying down on the fallen tree beside the lake. His gaze would always be fixed on something. Sometimes it's the mountains. Sometimes on the still lake. Or sometimes, on the children playing in the clearing. He belongs to a rural village near Pollachi. Some say that he was from a wealthy family who turned into an ascetic after a tragic incident. Some say that he is a runaway. In fact, there are many stories about him. Some of these stories include the way he cured a little boy of his inability to walk, the way he made a dumb woman speak, and so on. These are stories that everyone around here knows. These stories are a part of our everyday life. These stories make our life a little more interesting in fact. He makes our place special; this part of the estate is known for his unique skills of healing. Swami isn't an old man as you might think. Not someone with a religious garb either. He is an ordinary man, somewhere in his thirties. A very strong and healthy-looking man. And his eyes were always seeking something beyond what I could understand. That is the only thing that made him appear different.

Swami has always intrigued me with his silence. But unlike the mad man, Swami's silence was calming. He would always carry a walking stick and a knife with him. He would eat only if someone offered food. No one knows where he lives. These mountains are his home. He often smiles at Ammu. When he comes back from the town, he often brings her toffees. The girl is fond of him too.

By this age, there are a few things I have realised. After I am married off, Mathew sir won't have the strength to raise a child, that too, a girl child. His son won't have the sense to bring her up and my parents don't have the means to. And by no chance will my future husband agree to take care of someone else's child. I knew I would have to leave her one day. But upon all the Gods I pray to, I don't know where I will leave her. Her home is Vasanthi and Vasanthi is helpless. I am afraid I will have to leave her with strangers. Or even worse, in an orphanage. The very thought makes me shudder. For the first time in my life, I feel the pangs of anger. I am angry at the helplessness I face. I feel that life is unfair to those who are deprived of means.

Ammu would be four soon. She has long hair by

now. It is a joy to hear her anklets making sounds as she runs around. Her pet squirrel no longer visits the tree. It is winter and the mist covers the land like a blanket. December is the time when no one can make out what is right before them. For me, it is the best part of the year, when life comes to a near standstill and everyone prefers to stay home. Winter is the warmest month at home.

It was late in the night. The nine 'o'clock teleserial had just ended when we heard a knock on the door. My father rose to get the door, Amma behind him. It was Swami. And that was strange.

He had left the village a month ago. He didn't tell anyone where he was off to and no one had any means of talking to him after he left. That was the first time I saw him in three months, and he looked totally different. He was wearing a dhothi and a shawl over him. His long hair and his beloved stick were gone. To be honest, I was taken back; what could have happened to him that made him retract from a world of stillness.

"Are you okay Swami? What happened?" My father's voice was shivering in the cold.

Swami replied in a gentle voice and that was the first time anyone had heard him speak. He asked my father if he could stay here for the night. My father was overwhelmed by his request. He kept saying that it was a blessing to have him in our house. But to our surprise, there was another person with him. A woman. Swami gestured to the person standing behind him to come inside. Her name was Janani.

My parents were shocked to see that Swami had brought a woman with her. It made them extremely uncomfortable. It made them worried. But their reverence to the man left them silent. The gossip went all over the place that the ascetic has become a family man and versions of the story with added masalas were also going around well. But nothing had an effect on him. He smiled at all of them, just the way he used to.

The very next day after his return, Swami went to meet Mathew sir. They had a rather long conversation and he offered Swami a job. Swami started working in the estate as a daily wage labourer. He moved into their new house with Janani two days after they came back. She came out only to see him off as he left the house for work. And by the time they moved, both I and Ammu had become friends with Janani. It was Janani who told me why Swami married her. And after that, I have always bowed down to him in my heart.

Three months from that day, I left my home for my husbands'. But I was at peace. I cried, definitely. I was leaving my child behind. But Ammu somehow knew that it was okay for me to leave her. We made her believe that Janani was sick and that is why I had to raise her. As I walked to the Jeep with my things, I looked at Swami, who now smelled of the earth rather than of the ash. He smiled at me; his eyes were moist.

They were no longer fixed upon the mountains. They looked out for Ammu; he has become a parent now. As the vehicle started moving, I waved at my parents, and at Swami, who was waiting by the Gulmohar. But my heart was with my child, who now slept next to Janani. I smiled at Swami, thankfully, one last time before they all disappeared from my view.

on the way back home

Two women sat next to each other. One got on to the bus at Murinjapuzha. She was gasping for air as she sat down. The KSRTC was moving slower than usual today; the fog was dense. December is a tough month here. The winds are harsh, the rain merciless, and the roads much too full of gutters. No one could see a thing beyond ten metres; ten was actually stretching it too far; you could barely see a person standing a metre away. Even the drivers who know the road and its condition are always careful. They are responsible for a lot more lives than what the bus carried.

Mary leaves the office by five every day. Calculating the minutes before the KSRTC leaves the bus stop, she walks in haste. Sometimes she runs. She was forty-five, a mother, and like most women of her age, she was obese because she didn't have to bother about her looks. She rarely had time to take care of her health. Her knee joints were already struggling. She had the look of a person in constant struggle actually; not just physically but also emotionally. The lines on her forehead spoke in agreement as well. And at the bus stop, she was always worried whether she would get a seat as her legs would often complain about carrying her. She said a silent prayer every time she left the office.

The sky was dark from the clouds. It looked as though the sun hadn't been around for years. Everything looked grey; even the greenery around was covered in a tint of grey. This disturbed her. The darkness. Anu would be home by now; the school disperses at four. Mary couldn't help but think of what Anu would have for tea, whether she would turn off the gas properly or close the door as soon as she is home. She held many fears for her child. She was afraid of everything when it came to her only daughter. If she was late one day, it meant that the neighbours' phone would ring a thousand times before she reaches home. There was no one to look after Anu. Her father comes home late, and at times, he never turns up.

She shared her seat with a stranger today. Usually, it would be Lissy, the village office clerk. But she is on leave today since her son is back home. They would share stories, sometimes eat the fried groundnuts that Lissy buys from the Selvan chettan[9] or simply sit warm, looking out and admiring the view. Mary believed that the mountains had a way of healing people.

The stranger was wearing a bright yellow salwar, the kind you get only in towns. No one here adores bright hues; people are satisfied with the dullness that loomed in their lives. She noticed the young woman;

---

[9] Chettan refers to an elder brother, or someone older than oneself.

her ornaments, the shoes she wore, and the packet of tissues she held. It looked as though the woman was sneezing all the way, or perhaps was crying. Mary couldn't make out. Mary tried to smile at her.

She smiled at the young woman the way one smiles at strangers, and young woman returned a dim, half-alive smile. That granted Mary the freedom to look out and not bother about the near twenty-five, fair looking, young woman who kept crying in between. Things were normal between them. There was a boundary that made them both comfortable.

Her name was Tara. The kind of girl who stood out because of the finer qualities she owned. Her eyes were kind, and everyone talked about them. Her ability to weave words was appreciated everywhere. She had more well-wishers in her college than one would usually expect. No one held grudges against her and that was very rare in a college like theirs.

But life can change in a second. Even the strongest of beings can be shaken by the ways of life; fragility is a curse, I guess. Sometimes the winds hit us so hard that we lose our ground and stand lost. But then and there, a few lucky people find a grain of hope or so to hold on to. Blessed are the ones who did not have to give up.

Tara was in love, the kind of love in which you get lost blissfully. She wrote poems for him. A lot of them actually. Arun was the kind of person who made others realize that there is still hope left in this world.

They were celebrated; their love made everyone smile. But their love story did not end in smiles. It was nipped off before it bloomed. Destiny is not kind in the way we assume it to be. Once it takes away a part of us, that part remains hollow; sometimes forever. Life took away Arun from Tara.

And past all the mourning, today she decided to take a journey to her maternal home; this time without her mother. She left her mom yesterday and promised her that she would be back safe. Like Mary and Anu, Tara and her mother were the only families they had.

We don't often realize the common ground we share with the strangers we meet. We walk past them as if they don't belong in our lives. And Mary sat next to Tara, thinking that she was just another stranger. Mary looked at the beautiful lights from the sub-station at Vandiperiyar. It was almost six.

The silence between them was lightened only by the dull smile they shared. It was a smile of understanding now, and thus of relief. Sometimes our souls recognize the struggles we all go through and force the heart to extend a hug, which due to the fear of being misunderstood, often gets reduced to a smile.

Tara stood up when the bus stopped at Kumily. She looked out. It was past dusk, but not yet dark. The unfamiliarity of the place made her eyebrows go up. The bus stand was alive; a lot of people were getting down from different buses while the others were searching for their buses with huge luggage. A few others, who walked relaxed, looked as if their lives were too easy.

Mary signalled her to get down as people were waiting behind them. Once out of the bus, Tara greeted the stranger she had met with a warm smile, and Mary smiled back with concern on her face. And that smile made her find the very next KSRTC back to Ernakulam. Tara then suddenly knew that all mothers were made of similar material.

The fog-covered bus stand witnessed two lives that were touched by nothing but mere silence. It witnessed their relieved smiles. It witnessed their journeys being resumed with a bit of added hope that spoke volumes about the silence we share with the world. Sometimes, silence is the loudest we can ever speak.